A N

Dear readers,

I'm so excited that Hodder Children's Books
is publishing new editions of your favourite
titles in the Animal Ark Pets series.

I know from your letters how much you
enjoy sharing Mandy and James's love of
animals. As you can tell, I'm a huge fan of
animals myself and can't imagine a day
when I will ever want to stop writing about
them.

Happy reading!

With very best wishes,

Lucy

LUCY DANIELS

ANIMAL ARK PETS

Kitten
Crowd

Hodder
Children's
Books

a division of Hodder Headline Limited

Special thanks to Sue Welford
Thanks also to C. J. Hall, B. Vet. Med., M.R.C.V.S. for reviewing
the veterinary information contained in this book

Animal Ark is a trademark of Working Partners Ltd
Copyright © 1996 Working Partners Ltd
Created by Working Partners Limited, London W6 0QT
Original series created by Ben M. Baglio
Illustrations copyright © 1996 Paul Howard
Cover illustration by Chris Chapman

First published in Great Britain in 1996 by Hodder Children's Books

This edition published in 2006 by Hodder Children's Books

The right of Lucy Daniels to be identified as the Author of
the Work has been asserted by her in accordance with the
Copyright, Designs and Patents Act 1988.

For more information about Animal Ark,
please contact www.animalark.co.uk

1

A Catalogue record for this book is available from the British Library

ISBN 0 340 91783 0

Typeset in Bembo by Avon DataSet Ltd,
Bidford-on-Avon, Warwickshire

Printed and bound in Great Britain by
Clays Ltd, St Ives plc

The paper and board used in this paperback by Hodder Children's
Books are natural recyclable products made from wood grown in
sustainable forests. The manufacturing processes conform to the
environmental regulations of the country of origin.

Hodder Children's Books
a division of Hodder Headline Limited
338 Euston Road
London NW1 3BH

Contents

1

A problem for Mandy

"What's the hurry, Mandy?" Mr Simpson, the school caretaker, called after Mandy Hope as she ran helter-skelter down the corridor towards the front doors.

"I've been cleaning out the gerbils," Mandy said, out of breath. "And I forgot to tell James I'd be a bit late. He'll be wondering where I am!"

James Hunter was Mandy's best friend. They always rode their bikes home together. Helping with Terry and Jerry, the class gerbils, was one of Mandy's favourite things at school. She loved animals. Being allowed to help look after the school gerbils was almost like having pets of her very own.

By the main entrance door was the school bulletin board. You could put all sorts of notices up on the bulletin board. If you wanted to sell or buy anything, that was the place to let people know.

As she passed the board, one large notice caught Mandy's eye. She stopped to see what it said.

Does anyone want a free kitten? If so, tell Katie Greene, Class Four, or phone Welford 706354

"That's me," a voice said behind her. "I've just put that notice up."

Mandy turned to see a girl of about eight, a year younger than herself, staring at her.

"Are the kittens yours?" she asked.

Katie nodded. "We're moving house soon and Dad says we can only take their mother, Tibby, with us," she explained.

"Why?"

Katie looked sad. "He said seven cats is too many."

"Seven?" Mandy said.

"Yes, Tibby's got six babies," Katie explained.

"Oh," Mandy said. "I see. Seven cats *is* rather a lot I suppose."

"Would you like one?" Katie looked at Mandy hopefully.

Mandy shook her head. "I would *love* one but both my parents are vets. They're too busy looking after other people's animals for us to have a pet of our own."

Katie sighed. "I just don't know what's going to happen if we can't find homes for them."

Mandy's heart lurched. She could hardly bear to think of it. Six tiny kittens with no one to love and take care of them. "Maybe I can help you," she said quickly. "I'll ask all my friends."

"Oh, would you?" Katie said.

Mandy nodded. "And Mum and Dad might know someone. I'll ask as soon as I get home."

Katie's eyes shone. "Thanks."

Mandy made up her mind there and then. She would do everything she could to help Katie find homes for her kittens.

It wasn't going to be easy. Most people Mandy knew already had a pet. But she had lots of friends in the village. Surely some of them would like a kitten.

Mandy hitched her bag on to her shoulder. She went through the main doors out into the playground. Katie followed.

"Would you like to come round and see the kittens sometime?" she asked Mandy.

Mandy's eyes lit up. She couldn't refuse an offer like that.

"Oh, yes please," she said. "I'd really love to."

"I live along Meadow Lane," Katie said. "Number 16. It's just behind the church."

"I'll ask Mum and Dad if I can come this evening," Mandy said. "After tea? Will your parents mind?"

"No, of course not." Katie shook her head.

"Could I bring my friend, James?" Mandy asked. She knew James would love to see the kittens too.

"Would he like one, do you think?" Katie asked hopefully.

Mandy shook her head. "I'm afraid he's already got a cat. And a puppy."

Katie's face fell. "Oh, I guess not. See you later, then." She ran on ahead to get her bike, then rode off towards the church.

Mandy felt full of excitement. Six tiny kittens. She just couldn't wait to see them!

2

Free to a good home

James was waiting for Mandy by the bike shed. He had a worried look on his face.

James was a year younger than Mandy (he was in the same class as Katie). He and Mandy had been friends ever since Mandy had helped him choose his puppy, Blackie, from a litter of black Labradors.

"I thought you were *never* coming," James

called as Mandy hurried towards him. He hitched his schoolbag on to his shoulder and got on his bike.

"Race you home!" he called, pedalling off.

Mandy cycled quickly to catch him up. "Wait," she said. "I've got something important to tell you."

They rode side by side as Mandy told James about Katie's kittens.

"*Six*!" James exclaimed. He took one hand off the handlebars and pushed his glasses back on to the bridge of his nose. His bike wobbled. "That's not going to be easy."

"I know," Mandy said. "But I promised to try. Will you help me, James?"

"Course I will," James said. He loved animals almost as much as Mandy.

They cycled through the small village of Welford towards Animal Ark.

Animal Ark was the name of Mr and Mrs Hope's surgery, attached to the house where they lived.

Mandy usually won the race home from

school but today she lagged behind. Her mind was still on Katie's kittens.

"Come on, slowcoach," James called.

They reached James's house and stopped outside the gate. Blackie was looking out of the front window. He always watched for James to come home and he started barking excitedly when he saw them.

"Don't forget to ask your mum and dad about the kittens," Mandy reminded James.

"OK," James said. "I won't." He pushed open the front gate and went through. "I'll see you after tea."

"Yes, see you later."

Mandy waved as she pedalled quickly off towards Animal Ark.

When she got there, Mandy dumped her bike by the surgery entrance. She dashed inside. Jean Knox, the receptionist, was on the telephone.

Mandy wandered round looking at the notice board. Her heart sank. Several other people had kittens for sale. That would make it even more difficult to find homes for Katie's.

On the table was a pile of leaflets telling people how to take care of their pets. Mandy thumbed through them. Kittens, puppies, hamsters, gerbils, budgies, bunnies . . . there were hints on how to look after almost every kind of pet you could think of. The Hopes believed it was important for people to know how to take proper care of their animals.

As soon as Jean put down the receiver Mandy blurted out. "Can I see Mum and Dad? Are they here?"

Jean looked at Mandy over the top of her glasses. "I'm afraid your dad's gone out on a call. Your mum's here, though, if you want to see her."

Mandy rushed through into the surgery. Mrs Hope was packing away some medicines as Mandy came into the room. Her red hair was tied back and she wore a stethoscope round her neck. Her white vet's coat was draped across the examining table.

"Hi, Mandy," she said. "Had a good day at school?"

10

"Yes, fine, thanks," Mandy said quickly. She wanted to tell her mum about Katie's kittens. Her words seemed to tumble over themselves.

". . . and they're moving very soon so we haven't got long. Oh, Mum, we've got to do something to help!"

Mrs Hope smiled gently. "Now, calm down, Mandy. This will need a bit of thought."

She finished putting the boxes away and sat down. "Six kittens. Mandy, I don't know. It is an awful lot."

Mandy hoisted herself up on the examining table. "I know, but there must be *someone* in the village who wants them," she said. "And they *are* free."

"Yes, well," Mrs Hope said. "That will help, of course."

"And I could tell people how to look after them," Mandy added.

"Yes, I know you could," Mrs Hope said.

"James is going to ask his mum and dad," Mandy told Mrs Hope.

"Good. The more people that know, the better."

"What will happen if Katie can't find homes for them?" Mandy asked. She felt suddenly afraid. She hadn't see the kittens yet but she knew they would be sweet.

Mrs Hope looked glum. "I don't know, Mandy. It's not going to be an easy task, you know. Welford's only small and most people already have pets of one kind or another."

"I know," Mandy said sadly. "That's the trouble."

"You could put a notice up in the waiting-room, if you like," Mrs Hope said suddenly.

"Oh, Mum, can I?" Mandy's eyes shone. She jumped down. "I'll do it now."

"What will you do now?" said a voice from the doorway.

It was Mr Hope. He came in and put his bag down on the table.

Mandy gave him a hug and quickly explained about the kittens.

"I see." Mr Hope stroked his beard

thoughtfully. "And Katie wants to find homes for them all?"

"That's right," said Mrs Hope. "The whole lot!"

"Another pet rescue then," Mr Hope said. His eyes twinkled as he glanced at Mrs Hope. They were both quite used to Mandy's schemes to help pets.

"Looks like it," Mrs Hope replied.

"I know Katie's family," Mr Hope went on. "Mrs Greene brought Tibby to see me a few weeks before the kittens were born. She needed some vitamin shots. I'm sure they'll be grateful for your help, Mandy."

"I know Katie will be," Mandy said. "She was so worried about the kittens, Dad. I know it's not going to be easy but I've promised I'll do everything I can," she added. "And that's exactly what I'm going to do. Starting with that notice."

Mandy ran out to the waiting-room.

"Jean, could I borrow a marker pen and a piece of white card, please?"

"What on earth for?" Jean asked.

Mandy explained quickly.

"I see." Jean opened her drawer and took out the things Mandy needed.

Mandy sat on one of the chairs. She chewed the end of the pen and looked thoughtful. What should she put? Something that would *really* catch people's eyes. She began writing:

A WHOLE CROWD OF KITTENS
Six cute kittens
Free to a good home
Apply to
Katie Greene, 16, Meadow Lane,
or Mandy Hope at Animal Ark

Mandy handed the notice to Jean. "Would you pin this up on the board, please?"

Jean got a couple of drawing pins and went to pin up the card. She stood back to look.

"You're right, Mandy. It does stand out. 'A good home'," she quoted. "Are you hoping that *one* person will take the whole . . ." She chuckled ". . . crowd?"

Mandy sighed. "It would be nice if all the kittens stayed together, wouldn't it? It's going to be bad enough losing their mother, let alone being split up from their brothers and sisters."

Jean nodded. "Yes, but I don't know who on earth is going to have enough room for six kittens."

"No," Mandy said with a sigh. "Neither do I."

3

A box of kittens

Mandy was so excited about seeing the kittens she could hardly eat her tea. She sat at the table reading the class project sheet Mrs Todd, her teacher, had given her during the last lesson.

Mr Hope peered over Mandy's shoulder. "What's that you've got there?" he asked.

Mandy explained. "We've got to keep a diary."

"That'll be interesting," her dad said.

"Yes," Mandy said. "Then we've got to read them out to the class. Mrs Todd's giving a prize for the best one."

"I'm sure you'll have lots to put in yours," Mr Hope said. "There's never a dull moment here!"

Mandy grinned. "That's true."

She packed away her project sheet. She would have to start her diary later.

By the time Mandy had changed into her jeans it was almost six o'clock. She hurried along to James's house. She ran up the front path and knocked on the door. Blackie barked and doggie footsteps came thudding up the passageway.

James's door opened. Blackie pushed past and ran out, his tail wagging furiously as he saw Mandy. He gave a loud bark and started pulling at the laces of her shoes and making growling noises. Mandy chuckled and pushed him gently away. "Blackie!"

She bent down and hugged him tightly. "Now, Blackie!" she said more sternly. "I don't want shredded laces, thank you very much!"

She took hold of Blackie's collar. "Sit!" she commanded.

Blackie ignored her. He just barked again, then ran off round the side of the house. He stopped by the rose bed and started to dig.

James dashed after the puppy and grabbed his collar. He pulled him away from the rose bed and dragged him back indoors. He shut the door quickly before Blackie could run out again.

Mandy laughed. "You're not having much luck training him, are you?"

"No, 'fraid not," James said. "But I *am* trying."

"I think you've got a lot more work to do," Mandy giggled.

"Yes," James sighed. "You're right."

"Come on, then," Mandy said. "Let's go and see those kittens."

Mandy and James made their way along

the sleepy main street and across the village green.

A big man in a cloth cap was coming the other way. It was Walter Pickard. Mr Pickard had just retired from being the village butcher. He lived in one of the tiny cottages behind the village pub.

Walter's face lit up when he saw Mandy and James coming towards him.

"Hello, you two." His voice was deep and kindly. "Where are you off to in such a hurry?"

Mandy told him. "You don't want another cat, I suppose, Walter?" she asked hopefully. She knew Walter had three cats already. Surely one more wouldn't make much difference?

Walter shook his head. "Sorry, young miss. My three young'uns get up to enough mischief already, thank you."

"Never mind," Mandy sighed. "I just thought I'd ask."

Walter waved as they hurried on their way. They went along the narrow footpath beside the church. It was a short cut to Meadow Lane.

"Here we are," Mandy said as they reached Number 16. She pushed open the gate. James followed her down the path.

The house looked rather bare and empty. There weren't any curtains at the windows. Mandy guessed they had been taken down for the move. A couple of wooden packing cases stood outside the front door. There was a pile of newspapers beside them.

Just as Mandy was about to knock, Katie

came whizzing round the side of the house on her bike.

Her face lit up when she saw Mandy and James.

"Hiya," she said. "I was just going to see if you were coming." She got off her bike and propped it up against the fence. "Come on, they're round the back."

Round the back of the house was a tumbledown wooden shed. Katie pushed open the door.

Mandy peered in. She gave a shiver. It was damp and dark inside the shed. There were a lot of garden tools stacked up against the one wall and a lawn mower in the corner. There was only one small window to let in the light. Surely the mother cat and her kittens weren't in here?

Katie bent down and pulled aside a curtain covering the front of an old cupboard.

Mandy drew in her breath. There, in a cardboard box, was a small, rather thin, black cat. Nestled into her side were six tiny bundles of fur.

Mandy bent down with a little cry. "Oh, look, James. Aren't they gorgeous!"

Two of the kittens were black and two were ginger. The other two were ginger *and* black. They all had beautiful big eyes and tiny, screwed up faces.

James knelt beside Mandy. "They certainly are," he whispered.

"Does Tibby mind being stroked?" Mandy asked, looking up at Katie. She knew you had to be careful not to upset mother cats.

Katie shook her head. "No, she doesn't mind at all."

Katie knelt down beside Mandy and James. She picked up one of the ginger kittens. "Here." She gave it to Mandy. Then she picked up one of the black ones and gave it to James.

Mandy cradled the tiny creature against her chest. It mewed softly and clung to her. It had tiny, very sharp claws.

"They're so beautiful," Mandy whispered.

The sight of the six squirming, furry

creatures with their tiny ears and perfect little kitten faces made Mandy's heart turn over.

Tibby gave a small miaow as Mandy gently put the kitten back. She picked up one of the black and ginger ones and stroked it softly. She felt the tiny bones of its head and legs.

"Are you sure they're warm enough in here?" she asked Katie anxiously. She knew how important it was to keep kittens and their mothers as warm and dry as possible. She wasn't at all sure that the cats were being looked after properly.

"I kept them indoors in the cupboard under the stairs when they were first born," Katie explained. "But Mum has had to clear it out so we brought them out here. Mum says they're all right."

Mandy bit her lip. A damp old cardboard box was hardly all right! The kittens did look healthy enough but she would have felt happier if they were indoors in a warm room.

"How old are they?" she asked.

"Nearly six weeks," Katie said. "Will that be old enough for them to go to new homes?"

"Just about," Mandy said. "Most kittens are taken away from their mothers at six or seven weeks."

Katie sighed and looked sad. "I don't know what we're going to do with them. Did you ask your mum and dad?"

Mandy put the second kitten back and stood up. "Yes, they don't know anyone off-hand. But I've put a notice on our board," she added. "Maybe someone will see it at surgery tonight."

"Oh, I hope so," Katie said. "We're moving on Saturday."

"Saturday!" James exclaimed. "We'll *never* find homes by then."

Mandy frowned at him. "Yes, we will," she said firmly. "I know we will. We've got to!"

Before they went out, Mandy tucked the blanket carefully round the mother cat and her babies. She noticed that the feed bowls by the box were both empty.

"She needs some milk," she said. She picked up a bowl. "And she should have fresh water to drink whenever she wants it."

"Oh dear, I forgot to get some," Katie said. "I had to help Mum with the packing."

"Well, you can get some now, can't you?" Mandy said. She was determined not to go home until Tibby had fresh food and water.

Mandy wanted to find homes for six *healthy* kittens, not six *hungry* ones.

Mandy and James waited while Katie went indoors to fill up the dishes.

"I don't think they're very happy in here, do you?" James said, looking worried.

"No," Mandy said, "I don't." She looked angry. "People shouldn't have pets if they can't look after them properly."

"No, they shouldn't," James agreed.

"The sooner they've got a new home, the better," Mandy added. "And it's up to us to find it for them."

"Have you asked your Gran and Grandad if they know anyone?" James asked.

Mandy shook her head. "No, but we'll pop in on the way home. Gran knows *everyone*, so maybe she'll have some ideas."

4

A brilliant idea

Mandy and James said goodbye to Katie at the front gate.

"I'll see you at school tomorrow," Mandy said. "Maybe we'll have some news about the kittens by then."

"I hope so," Katie said with another sigh.

Mandy and James made their way up the hill to Lilac Cottage where Gran and

Grandad lived. Their car was in the drive. Grandad's bike was leaning up against the wall.

Grandad was in the garden tidying up the flower borders. He grinned when he saw Mandy and James coming up the path.

"Hi, you two." He stood up and pushed his cap to the back of his head. "Gran's baking cakes. You must have smelled them."

Mandy ran to give her grandad a hug. "Gran's *always* just baked something," she said.

"True," Grandad laughed. "She's gone mad today, though. Baked enough for an army."

"Is there a village fête or something, then?" James asked.

Grandad shook his head. "No, they're for Westmoor House, the old folks' home. One of the residents is a hundred years old this week and they're having a party."

"Wow!" said James. His eyes were wide behind his glasses. "A hundred!"

"I bet she's baked a hundred cakes,

then," Mandy said, laughing. "Let's go and see."

Gran was in the kitchen surrounded by trays of cakes and a mountain of washing up. She gave Mandy a kiss.

"Sit down, you two," she said. "I'll just finish drying up then I'll find you both some lemonade."

"We'll help, won't we, James?" Mandy took a tea cloth from its rack by the cooker.

"Oh, will we?" James had already sat down at the table and was gazing hungrily at the buns.

"Yes." Mandy took another cloth and put it in front of him. He got up with a sigh and started drying some of the dishes.

"Where have you been, Mandy?" Gran asked. She dried her hands, then went over to the fridge. She got out a jug of home-made lemonade and put it on the table.

Mandy explained about the kittens. "Why don't you have one, Gran?" she said. "They're so sweet and it wouldn't be *any* trouble."

Gran shook her head. "I'm sorry, Mandy. You know how we love going away on holiday and we'd hate to be tied down with a pet."

"I'd always look after it if you were away," Mandy said.

Gran shook her head again. "Sorry, Mandy. If you own a pet you have to be responsible for it yourself, not rely on other people."

Mandy sighed. Gran was right, of course. You *did* have to be responsible for your own pets.

She dried the last of the cake tins and sat down, her chin on her hands. "You're right, Gran. But will you ask your friends?"

Gran gave her a hug. "Yes, of course I will. Don't look so down in the dumps. Something will turn up."

"What will turn up, Dorothy?" Grandad came in and went to wash his hands at the sink.

"Homes," Mandy said. "Homes for kittens."

"Oh." Grandad reached out for one of Gran's fresh baked biscuits.

Gran slapped his fingers. "Hands off!" she said sharply. "There won't be enough for the party."

"Spoilsport." Grandad smiled just the same. He looked at the clock. "I'm going to watch the cricket on television. Coming, James?"

"Er . . ." James seemed reluctant although he loved cricket. He was still eying the cakes hopefully.

"Oh, here you are," Gran said, handing

him a chocolate bun. "And help yourself to lemonade."

"Thanks, Mrs Hope!" James said.

"Don't forget we've got to load all these into the car and take them over to Westmoor House," Gran called as Grandad disappeared into the front room. James followed, a glass of lemonade in one hand, his half-eaten bun in the other.

"I won't," Grandad called back. "Just let me know when you're ready."

Mandy still sat at the table, looking glum.

"Cheer up, Mandy," Gran said. She began packing the cakes and biscuits into tins. "How long have you got to find homes for these kittens?"

"Only a couple of days." Mandy was beginning to feel desperate. "They're moving on Saturday."

"Saturday!" Gran put a bun on a plate and gave it to Mandy. "We'd better get a move on then, hadn't we?"

"Yes," Mandy said. She took a bite of the bun. It was delicious.

"Well, I'm going to a WI meeting later

this evening once I've delivered these goodies to Westmoor House. I'll ask everyone at the meeting if you like."

"Thanks, Gran, you're brilliant!"

Gran peered at Mandy over the top of her glasses. "Well, we'll see about that. Don't count your chickens before they're hatched."

"Don't count your kittens, you mean," Mandy said.

When all the cakes and biscuits were packed away Mandy and James helped put them in the car.

"We could drop you off on the way, if you like," Grandad said. "I need to pop in to see your dad anyway, Mandy. Want a lift too, James?"

"Yes, please."

They dropped James off first. Blackie was standing with his nose through the gate.

"That puppy gets bigger every day," Gran said, waving goodbye to James.

"And naughtier," Mandy said. "See you tomorrow," she called as James went up the path with Blackie at his heels.

When they got to Animal Ark, Mrs Hope was just going out on an emergency call.

"Dad's had to go out too," she said as she came through the gate. "I was just coming to find you, Mandy."

"She can come with us, if you like," Gran said through the car window. "Then we'll stay with her until you get back."

"I'd be really grateful," Mrs Hope said. "Is that all right, Mandy?"

"Fine," Mandy said. She turned to her gran. "I'll help you unload the cakes, if you like."

"That would be a great help," Gran said.

Westmoor House was about a mile outside of the village. It was a big Victorian house which had recently been turned into an old people's nursing home. There were twenty-four residents so far.

Grandad drove up to the front door. Mandy got out and rang the bell. A woman opened the door. She was tall and slim and wore a grey suit.

The woman looked surprised to see Mandy standing on the doorstep.

"My gran and grandad have brought the cakes for the party," she explained.

"Oh, lovely," the woman said. "I'm Della Skilton, the home's manager. Pleased to meet you, Mandy."

Mandy helped Gran and Grandad take the tins through to the kitchen.

"I'm so grateful," Della said. "Our residents will really appreciate it."

Mandy looked around. There was a huge cooker at one end of the kitchen. She supposed you needed a big one when you had to cook for so many people every day.

Through the window, Mandy could see a long garden with lawns and flower beds. There were two old ladies sitting in deck-chairs enjoying the warmth of the evening sunshine.

"When's the party?" Mandy asked.

"On Friday. It's going to be a big surprise for Mrs Brown."

"I love parties," Mandy said. "Especially surprise ones."

"Why don't you come after school?" Della said. "You could help us hand round the food. Everyone would love to meet you, I'm sure."

"I'd love to," Mandy said. Then she remembered the kittens. Friday was the day before Katie moved. Mandy might still be busy searching for a home for them.

"Oh . . . but I'm sorry, I'll be really busy on Friday. I'd like to come another day, though, if I could."

Della smiled. "Come any time, Mandy.

The residents love to see young people. Some of them don't have any families, you see. And even though they all live together here some of them feel quite lonely."

Mandy felt sad. It must be horrible not to have anyone of your own. She was lucky. She had her mum and dad, and her grandparents. She had James too and other friends at school. Then there were Blackie and Benji, Walter's cats, Tom and Jerry the gerbils and all the other animals she knew. They were her friends too.

"I'll come as soon as I can," she said. "Would that be all right, Gran?"

Gran smiled. "Yes, of course it would, Mandy. You could bring James too, I expect."

"James is my best friend," Mandy told Della.

When all the cakes had been taken inside, Della went with Mandy and her grandparents to the door.

"Have a lovely party," Mandy said. "Will there be lots of presents?"

"Oh, I'm sure there will," Della said.

When they arrived back at Animal Ark, Mandy's parents were still out.

"It must be almost your bedtime," Gran said as they went in through the back door. "You run up and get ready and I'll make you a warm drink. Then I must be off to my meeting."

"Thanks, Gran." Mandy kissed her gran then ran upstairs to change into her pyjamas. She took her big old teddy bear off the bed and gave him a hug.

Mandy's schoolbag was on the chair. She took out her project sheet and gazed at it thoughtfully. She would have a lot to write in her diary today: finding out about the kittens; going to see them; then calling at Westmoor House. She would write it before she went to sleep. Maybe tomorrow she might find homes for the kittens.

Now that really would be something to put in her diary.

Downstairs, Grandad was watching TV. Mandy went and sat on the floor by his feet. She sipped her hot chocolate. Gran made the best hot chocolate!

Mandy was still thinking about the kittens. She just could not get the sweet, furry creatures out of her mind.

Suddenly Grandad gave a great laugh at the television. "Pat-dogs!" he exclaimed. "Have you ever heard of such a thing?"

"Pat . . . what?" Mandy said.

"Pat-dogs," Grandad repeated. "They're taking dogs into hospitals and nursing homes so that the patients can pat them."

Mandy frowned. "What do you mean?"

"Well," Grandad said, "someone said that people feel much happier if they have pets to love and cuddle. So that's what they're doing. They're introducing good-natured dogs into places to make the residents and patients feel better."

Mandy drew in her breath. What a fantastic idea! *Everyone* knew how happy you felt if you had a pet to cuddle.

Mandy suddenly thought of the old people at Westmoor House. *They* would love to have a pet to care for.

Mandy's heart began to race. She'd just thought of something. If you could have pat-dogs, why not pat-*cats?*

She turned her face towards her grandad, her eyes shining. "Grandad," she said. "I've just had the most fantastic idea!"

5

Mandy's plan

"But don't you see?" Mandy said when she had finished telling Grandad her idea. "I bet the old people would love to have pat-cats. They would make them feel *much* better."

"I'm sure you're right, Mandy," Grandad said. "The cats would be great company for the old folks. But *six*? Surely they wouldn't want the whole crowd?"

"There's twenty-four people there," Mandy insisted. "That's only a quarter of a cat each."

Grandad laughed. "I can see you've been practising your sums, Mandy Hope."

"That doesn't take much working out," Mandy said.

"Why don't you ask Della then?" Grandad suggested. "There's no harm in asking. You know what your gran always says. If you don't ask, you don't get."

Mandy jumped to her feet. "I'll ring her right now!"

Grandad got up too. "Not now, young lady. It's your bedtime. You'll have to do it tomorrow."

"But, Grandad!"

Grandad shook his head. "Sorry, Mandy. Rules: early to bed on school nights. One day won't make any difference. You'll get me shot if your mum comes home and you're still up and talking on the phone."

Mandy sighed. "OK, Grandad. I'll ring tomorrow."

Upstairs, Mandy sat in bed. She tried to start writing her diary, but she only got as far as putting "Day 1". She couldn't concentrate at all. Her mind kept wandering back to the kittens. She kept seeing them in that tatty old cardboard box. She kept smelling that musty old shed. What if Della didn't think pat-cats were a good idea after all? There were only two days left. Where else could she start looking?

The next day Mandy couldn't wait for school to be over.

She had told Mum and Dad her plan at the breakfast table. Mrs Hope had looked doubtful.

"How will they cope with six kittens?" she said. "Grown up cats are a different thing altogether. But six kittens could cause problems."

"There's a big garden," Mandy said. "They could play out there."

"Well," Mrs Hope said, "you'd better wait and see what Della says before you get your hopes up. But, Mandy . . ." She gazed at her daughter's excited face. "Don't be too disappointed if she says 'No', will you?"

"I won't," Mandy said although she knew she would be.

When it was time to go, James was waiting for Mandy by the front gate. She told him her plan as they cycled to school.

"That would be brilliant," he said.

"We could put our pocket money together and buy them a dish each." Mandy had been making plans in her head ever since she woke up. "And I'm sure Grandad will make them a big box if we ask him nicely."

"I'm sure my mum could find them an old blanket," James said. "One that Blackie hasn't chewed."

"Mum says they might not be able to cope with all six," Mandy said. "But I *would* like the family to stay together, if they can. Wouldn't you?"

"Yes." James looked thoughtful. "We could help, couldn't we? We could go there after school and feed them . . . things like that. Your mum could tell us what to do."

"I *know* how to look after kittens," Mandy said. "They need a warm bed and food and they need to be groomed every day. They need toys and . . ."

"There you are, then," said James. "No problem."

Mandy looked at him. "Della did say we could go and visit any time we like. James, you're brilliant!"

Katie was coming along the pavement as they arrived at school.

"Did anyone ring about the cats?" Mandy asked anxiously.

Katie shook her head sadly. "No. Have you found anybody?"

Mandy glanced at James. It would be better not to say anything until she had asked Della.

"No," Mandy said. "But my gran's going to ask around, and Mum and Dad."

"And my mum and dad," James added.

In class, Mrs Todd had to remind Mandy several times that gazing out of the window would not help her learn her maths.

"What's the matter with you, Mandy?" she asked when lessons were over. "You're not yourself today."

"I'm sorry, Mrs Todd," Mandy said. "I've got a lot on my mind."

"Yes, well make sure it's school work that's on your mind tomorrow," Mrs Todd said. "Otherwise you're going to get behind. We don't want that, do we?"

"No, Mrs Todd." Mandy hung her head. She knew it would be hard to set her mind to *anything* until she had found a place for the kittens. She just couldn't wait to get home and ring Westmoor House.

Katie caught up with Mandy just as she was leaving. "No one wants the kittens," she said. Mandy could see she was almost crying. "I've asked everybody." A tear ran down Katie's cheek. "And my dad says he's going to get rid of them."

"Get rid of them?" Mandy asked in horror. "What does he mean?"

Katie shrugged. "I don't know. He just said if they're not gone by Saturday

morning he'll get rid of them."

Mandy put her arm round Katie's shoulders. "Don't cry, Katie," she said. "James and I have got a plan."

"What kind of a plan?" Katie asked.

"I can't tell you yet," Mandy told her. "But I promise I'll let you know about it as soon as I can."

"We need to do something soon." Katie wiped her nose with the back of her hand. "Or it's going to be too late." She began to cry even harder. "It's bad enough having to leave all my friends," she sobbed. "But leaving the kittens as well . . ."

Mandy took a tissue from her bag. She gave it to Katie. The little girl blew her nose loudly.

"I'd better get home or Mum will wonder where I am."

"Try not to worry," Mandy said as they went to get their bikes.

Katie sniffed again. "I'll try. And thank you for helping me so far." She looked sad as she rode off in the direction of the church.

Mandy felt very anxious as she rode home with James. It was all right telling Katie not to worry. But how was she going to stop worrying herself?

"Can't stop," Mandy said as they arrived at James's gate. "I want to call Della as soon as I can."

"Good luck," James said.

"I'll let you know what she says," Mandy called as she rushed off. "Keep your fingers crossed."

"I will!" James shouted.

Mandy skidded to a halt outside her gate and flung it open. She propped her bike up against the wall and hurried in through the waiting-room door of Animal Ark.

Mrs McFarlane from the post office was sitting on one of the chairs. She had a cage on her lap. Inside it was a green budgie with all its feathers fluffed up. It looked very upset about something.

"Oh dear." Mandy stopped in her tracks. She sat down next to Mrs McFarlane and peered at the bird. "What's wrong with Sparky?" She put her finger through the bars. Sparky ignored it.

"I don't know," said Mrs McFarlane. "He's been like this for a couple of days."

"Maybe he's lonely," Mandy suggested. "Perhaps he would like a friend?"

Mandy *very* nearly suggested a kitten then thought better of it. Budgies and kittens definitely did not mix!

Mrs McFarlane sighed. "A mate, you mean?"

"Yes," Mandy said. "Budgies live in flocks in the wild. Most people only have one but they do like having a friend."

"You could be right," Mrs McFarlane said. "I'll see what your mum says, Mandy. He's been quite content with talking to himself in his mirror up to now."

Mandy stood up. "You don't know anyone who wants a kitten, do you?"

"I've already asked," Jean Knox said as she came in from the back room.

"I'm sorry, Mandy, I don't," Mrs McFarlane said. "I don't think poor Sparky would take kindly to a kitten."

"No," Mandy said. "Neither do I."

"I'll ask my customers if you like," Mrs McFarlane offered. "Most people come in at some time or other."

"It's got to be soon," Mandy said.

"I'll do my best," Mrs McFarlane promised.

"Has anyone else seen my notice?" Mandy asked Jean.

"One or two people," Jean said. "That's all I'm afraid."

"Not to worry," Mandy said. "If I'm

lucky I might find a home for them all this evening."

"Oh?" Jean raised her eyebrows. "All of them?"

"Yes," Mandy said with a grin. "The whole lot!"

Mandy dashed on through into the house. She dumped her bag in the hall and quickly looked up the number of Westmoor House. She keyed it in, tapping her fingers on the table.

"Please hurry," she muttered under her breath. "Please . . ."

But when someone did answer it wasn't Della.

"I'm afraid she's out," the voice said.

"Oh." Mandy's heart sank. Every minute was precious. Every passing hour took the kittens closer and closer to being "got rid of".

"When will she be back?" Mandy asked anxiously.

"About seven, I think," the voice told her. "Can I give her a message?"

Mandy thought it would be much better

to talk to Della herself. "No," she said quickly. "I'll try later, thank you."

Mandy put the phone down with a sigh. She looked at the clock on the wall. Two and a half hours! How on earth was she going to be able to wait that long?

Mandy was sitting at the kitchen table writing her diary when Mrs Hope came in from the surgery.

Mandy looked up. "Did you find out what was wrong with Sparky?" she asked.

"He just needed a tonic," Mrs Hope said. "And you'll be pleased to know Mrs McFarlane is going to get him a friend."

Mandy smiled. "That's great, Mum."

Mrs Hope went to put the kettle on. "Had a good day at school, Mandy?"

"No, terrible," Mandy said. "I've been thinking about Katie's kittens all day."

"Have you rung Westmoor House?" her mum asked.

Mandy nodded and told her what had happened.

Mrs Hope came up with a solution. "I

know," she said. "I've got to deliver some antibiotics to Syke Farm later. Why don't we call in at Westmoor House on the way?"

Mandy jumped up and gave her mum a hug. It would be *much* better to ask about the kittens in person.

"Oh, Mum, that would be brilliant! Can James come?" She knew James would hate to be left out.

"If his mum says it's OK," Mrs Hope said. "Ring and ask if you like."

James *did* want to come. He was waiting by his gate when Mrs Hope drew up later in the Land-rover. She opened the door.

"Hop in," she said.

"Thanks." James clambered into the back seat.

"I can't wait to see Della," Mandy told him excitedly. "Mum thinks pat-cats are a great idea, don't you, Mum?"

Mrs Hope nodded. "Yes, but it's Della you've got to convince, not me."

They arrived at the home just as Della pulled up in her car. She smiled when she saw Mandy.

"Not more cakes?" she said, her blue eyes twinkling.

"No," Mandy laughed. "We've come to ask you a favour."

"Oh?" Della said.

Mandy quickly introduced her mum then started to explain what they had come for. All her words seemed to come out too quickly.

". . . and you see we thought the old people would love them, didn't we, James?" she blurted out.

"Yes," James said, blinking up at Della.

Della held up her hand. "I think you'd better come inside and start all over again," she said.

When they got inside, Della took Mrs Hope, Mandy and James into her office.

"Do sit down," she said. "Now, Mandy, your friend Katie has got six unwanted kittens . . . right, now carry on."

Mandy finished the story.

"And Katie's dad is going to get rid of them," she said desperately. "Tomorrow!"

Della looked thoughtful. "Six cats." She

shook her head slowly. "Mandy, it's an awful lot."

"Maybe you could just take two," James said. "Or three . . . or . . ."

"But we would *really* like them all to stay together," Mandy said quickly. "Wouldn't we, James?"

"Yes," James agreed.

Della sat with her hands clasped together.

"It would be horrible for them to be split up," Mandy went on. "You said some of the people in here were sad because they didn't have families. I know they would understand how the kittens feel."

Della got up out of her chair. "Yes, you're right, Mandy. Well, let's go and ask some of the residents, shall we? Let's see what *they* think about having some pat-cats!"

6

A vote

Della took Mandy, James and Mrs Hope down a long carpeted corridor. There was a big room at the end. The buzz of talking and the sound of a television turned up loud came from inside.

Della opened the door and ushered them in. The room was full of people doing all sorts of things.

Four elderly gentlemen sat at a small table playing cards. In one corner several people were watching television. A very old man was asleep in a chair by the wide bay window and two ladies sat nearby reading newspapers.

Everyone looked up as they came in. Mandy felt suddenly shy as all eyes turned towards her. She reached up and gripped her mum's hand.

Della went across the room and turned down the television.

"Excuse me, everybody," she said in a loud voice. "I've got a young lady here who wants you to hear an idea she has."

Della took Mandy's hand and led her to the centre of the room. "Now, Mandy, why don't you tell everyone what you've just told me."

Mandy suddenly felt very nervous. Everyone was staring at her. One or two people began to mutter among themselves.

Mandy threw her mum a pleading glance. Mrs Hope nodded encouragingly.

"Go on, Mandy," she said. "This is your big chance."

Her mum was right. This was her big chance. Perhaps it was her *only* chance to save six precious little lives.

She cleared her throat. "Um . . ." she began. "I was watching TV with my grandad . . ."

"You'll have to speak up, dear." A loud voice came from an old lady in the corner. "Some of us are a bit hard of hearing."

Mandy shuffled her feet. "Sorry," she said.

Then, in a bold voice, Mandy told the story of the kittens. She told everyone how she had heard about pat-dogs from her grandad.

". . . and I thought," she said when she had almost finished, "that a great big house like this *should* have some pets." She turned round to look at all the people watching her. "And all those empty laps should have a cat on them," she added as an afterthought.

Everyone laughed and clapped their hands.

"Hear, hear," said one of the old gentlemen who had been playing cards. "I used to have a black moggy. I still miss him."

"Me too," said a lady by the television. She had put down her knitting to listen to Mandy. "I'd love a pat-cat." She turned to her friend, a tiny lady in a floral dress. "How about you, Dora?" she shouted in her ear.

Dora nodded and smiled at Mandy.

"I hate cats," one of the men suddenly piped up. "Noisy and smelly. Got fleas, all of 'em."

Mandy's heart sank. Supposing other residents felt the same?

"Oh, George." Della went to sit on the arm of the man's chair. "They would be very well-behaved, I'm sure."

The old man screwed up his nose. "Hate 'em," he mumbled.

Suddenly a very old lady sitting with her legs up on a stool spoke loudly. "Well, I adore cats," she said. "So you can be quiet, George."

"Hear, hear," said someone else. "Be quiet, George, why don't you?"

Mandy felt a bit sorry for George. He was only telling everybody how he felt.

Della rose and came over to Mandy. "That's Mrs Brown," she explained. "She's the one who's a hundred years old tomorrow."

"Oh," Mandy whispered. She just couldn't imagine what it felt like to have lived for a hundred years.

"Come and meet her."

Della took Mandy and James over to Mrs Brown. She introduced them and they shook hands.

Mrs Brown had the palest, most wrinkled face Mandy had ever seen. She gazed at Mandy with kindly, pale blue eyes.

"You love animals, do you dear?" she asked in a soft, wavering voice.

"Oh, yes," Mandy breathed. "So does James."

"And so do I," Mrs Brown said. "I've had lots of pets in my time and I really miss them." She gazed up at Della. "Why don't we take a vote on it, Della?"

"Good idea." Della marched back into the centre of the room and clapped her hands. Everyone fell silent again. "All those in favour of pat-cats raise your hands."

Mandy held her breath. A forest of hands rose into the air. Mandy gave a sigh of relief. It looked as if almost everyone like the idea.

"Against?" Della said.

Two people put up their hands. One was

George, the man who hated cats. Mrs Brown frowned at him. He put his hand down sharply and began mumbling to himself.

The only other person who objected was a man whose name was Tom. He had been asleep in the corner and had only woken up halfway through the voting.

"Don't worry about Tom," Della said. "He always objects to everything." She smiled at Mandy and James. "There you are then! It looks as if your kittens have found a home."

Mandy clapped her hands together.

"Oh, thank you, Della!" Mandy looked round. "Thank you everybody!" She ran to hug her mum. "Mum, isn't it great?"

Mrs Hope looked very pleased. "It certainly is, Mandy."

James was so overjoyed he couldn't speak. He just stood and grinned.

"I know you'll love them," Mandy said to Mrs Brown.

"Yes, dear. I'm really looking forward to seeing these kittens of yours."

"They're not mine," Mandy said with a chuckle. "They're yours!"

They left the old people talking excitedly. Della went with them to the front door.

"I'm a bit worried about finding the time to look after them," she said.

"They're only six weeks old," Mrs Hope said. "They'll still need quite a bit of care."

"James and I have got it all worked out," Mandy said hastily. "We'll come up every day after school and help you. Would that be all right?"

"That would be wonderful, Mandy," Della said. "Is that all right with you, Mrs Hope?"

"I don't want you neglecting your school work, Mandy," Mrs Hope said.

"I won't, honestly. In fact helping out with the kittens could be *part* of my school work."

"What do you mean?" Della looked puzzled.

Mandy explained about the diary.

"I'll keep a *kitten* diary," she said. "When

I've been up to visit them I'll write all about them and how they're getting on. I'll make a special copy for the residents."

"What a clever daughter you've got, Mrs Hope," said Della.

Mandy's mum rolled her eyes. "Yes, don't I know it!"

"When will you bring the kittens over?" Della asked.

"Tomorrow, if that's all right," Mandy said.

"Right, then, I'll look forward to seeing you. Oh, by the way," Della added. "Will they need injections of any sort?"

"They'll need injections against cat flu when they're a bit older," Mandy said before Mrs Hope had time to answer. "And they'll need some worm tablets too later on."

"Don't worry," Mrs Hope assured Della. "Bring them to the surgery when they're around three months old and I'll see to it."

"Thanks." Della opened the door for them. "I'll make a special place for the kittens by the stove in the kitchen. Thank you, Mandy. I think you've made a lot of people here very happy."

"Thank *you*," Mandy said. "See you tomorrow!"

"'We *are* going to have an exciting day," Della commented. "A birthday party *and* six new residents."

Mandy hummed as they drove back towards the village. The sun was going down and the sky looked like a red blanket.

Mandy thought about the kittens, curled

up with their mother in that damp shed in Katie's garden. Soon they would all have a lovely new home and lots of people to cuddle them.

Mandy knew the old folks would love them all. Even George!

By the time they had called at Syke Farm it was getting dark.

"You can ring Katie as soon as we get in," Mrs Hope said as they dropped James off and headed towards Animal Ark. "She'll be as pleased as punch, I'm sure."

But when Mandy dialled Katie's number all she got was a strange tone.

Mr Hope listened. "That means the phone has been cut off," he said. "It must be because they're moving in the morning. If you go round early you're bound to catch them," he told Mandy. "It takes ages to load those furniture vans."

But Mandy's heart turned over with fear. What if they were too late? What if Katie's father had already carried out his threat?

What if he had "got rid" of the kittens

before Mandy and James could pick them up?

Mandy thought tomorrow couldn't come soon enough.

7

Six missing kittens

"We're too late. They've gone!"

Mandy's hand flew to her mouth as she and James ran down the front path of Katie's house the following morning.

The house was all closed up, silent and empty. The family had left.

Blackie pulled excitedly at his head. Even an empty house was an adventure to him.

Mandy banged on the front door. The sound echoed down the deserted hall. Mandy's heart pounded. There was no one there. Now what were they going to do?

A man came out of the house next door.

"They've gone," he told Mandy and James. "Loaded the van last night and left about an hour ago."

"Did they take the kittens?" Mandy asked anxiously.

"Kittens?" the man said. Then he shrugged. "I don't know anything about any kittens."

"Let's go and look in the shed," James said.

They pushed open the side gate and ran round the path. The shed door was open.

James peered inside. "It's no good," he said. "They're not here. I wonder what they've done with them?"

Mandy sat down on the back step and burst into tears. "I don't know," she sobbed. She couldn't bear to think what might have happened to the kittens. "And what are we going to tell Della? The old people will be so upset."

James sat beside her, looking glum. Blackie had gone into the shed. They could hear him scrabbling about. Then he came out with a piece of old blanket in his mouth.

James grabbed it. "Leave!" he commanded. Blackie growled. He hung on more tightly than ever. He shook the piece of rag as if it were a rat.

"Blackie!" James said sternly.

At last Blackie let it go.

"It's the kittens' blanket," Mandy said, crying even harder.

"Maybe they've taken them with Tibby after all?" James tried to cheer Mandy up. "If they couldn't find homes for them?"

Mandy shook her head. "No. Katie said her dad was going to get rid of them. But where, that's what I'd like to know."

Blackie came to lick the tears off Mandy's cheeks. She buried her face in his soft fur.

After a while Mandy stopped crying. She stood up and squared her shoulders. Crying wouldn't bring the kittens back.

She and James would just have to go and explain to Della what had happened.

"We'd better go and tell Mum first," Mandy sniffed. "She was going to examine the kittens before we took them to Westmoor House. She'll be wondering where we've got to."

Mandy and James made their way back across the green towards Animal Ark.

The postman, Bill Ward, had just pulled up in his van outside the newsagents. He stopped there every morning to get his daily newspaper.

"You two look a bit glum," he said when he saw Mandy and James. "What's up?"

"We've lost six kittens," James said.

"Six kittens?" Mr Ward looked surprised "How on earth can you lose six kittens?"

Mandy explained.

"That's funny," Mr Ward said. "I passed John Greene's car this morning. It was right up the moorland road. I wondered what he was doing up there at the crack of dawn. Where were they moving to, do you know?"

Mandy shook her head. "No. It was a long way away because Katie has got to go to a new school. Was there a furniture van with them?"

"No, I just saw his car heading for the moors." Bill shook his head. "Seems a bit odd to go for a spin the day you're moving house." He shrugged. "Oh, well, people are strange sometimes."

He said goodbye to Mandy and James and drove off.

Mandy watched him go with a frown on her face. She knew that narrow moorland road. It led right up to High Tor. She had been up there a few times with her mum and dad. They hadn't been going for a drive though. They had been going up there for a special reason.

She turned to James. "Quick!" she gasped. "I bet I know where Mr Greene was going."

"Where?" James called as Mandy hurried on ahead. He dashed after her, Blackie pulling at the lead.

Mandy had already reached her house. Mr Hope was in the drive cleaning the mud off his Land-rover.

"Dad!" Mandy said breathlessly. "Are you busy?"

"Not really," Mr Hope said. "I'm off duty this morning."

"Could you take us up to the Welford Animal Sanctuary, please?"

Mr Hope frowned. "What on earth for? I thought you were supposed to be collecting those kittens."

"We are," Mandy said. "But when we got to Katie's house everyone had gone."

"Gone? What about the kittens?"

"I've got a feeling Mr Greene might have taken them up to the sanctuary. Please, Dad," Mandy urged. "Can we go and see?"

Mr Hope opened the car door. "We certainly can," he said. "Hop in, you two."

Mandy's heart thudded as Mr Hope drove through the village. He headed up the moorland road towards the Welford Animal Sanctuary. The sanctuary was run by a woman called Betty Hilder. She took in all kinds of unwanted and abandoned animals. It would be just the place to take the kittens.

When they reached the sanctuary a donkey in the field next to Betty's bungalow brayed a greeting. The sound of dogs barking came from the row of kennels behind the house.

Mandy ran up the path and rang the doorbell.

"I'm here," a voice called from one of the barns.

Betty came out to greet them. "Hello, Mandy, what brings you here?"

Mr Hope and James got out of the car. They all began talking at once.

"Well," she said when they had finished. "As a matter of fact . . ." she paused in mid sentence. "Better still, come and see for yourselves."

Betty led them round to the back door. She opened it and they followed her inside. She took them through to the kitchen. In front of the stove was a cardboard box.

"There," Betty said. " Are they what you're looking for by any chance?"

Mandy's heart was in her mouth as she ran across and kneeled down. There, all curled round and sleepy, were the six tiny kittens.

Mandy let out a sob of relief. "James, Dad, it's them! Oh, thank goodness!"

James ran and kneeled beside her. "It's them all right," he said to Mr Hope. "Come and see."

Mr Hope took out one of the kittens. It made a soft mewing noise. Mr Hope

frowned. "This one's a bit thin," he said.

Betty came to kneel beside them. "Yes, they all are. I found them on the doorstep when I got up this morning. They've had some warm milk already but they'd probably like some more." She went to heat some milk on the stove.

Mr Hope was examining the other kittens.

"They are all right, aren't they, Dad?" Mandy asked anxiously. "I had the feeling they weren't being looked after very well."

Her dad nodded. "They need to put on a bit of weight. They're all healthy enough but they're going to need special care for a few days."

"Oh dear," Mandy said, her heart sinking. "Della's very busy with the party and everything."

"Della?" Betty came back with the milk. She poured it into three saucers.

Mandy and James placed the kittens, two by two, in front of them. They began lapping the milk up. Their tiny tongues flicked in and out so fast they were just a blur.

Mandy explained about Westmoor House.

"How wonderful," Betty said. "I'm so pleased the kittens are going to stay together. They're such a dear little family."

"But I don't know how Della's going to find time to give them special care." Mandy sounded worried.

"I'd look after them myself," said Betty, "but we've got a full house at the moment."

Mr Hope was stroking his beard thoughtfully. "Maybe we could have them at Animal Ark for a while," he said.

Mandy drew in her breath. Six kittens at the surgery! Six kittens for her to look after. It would be like a dream come true.

"Oh, Dad!" she cried. "Could we really?"

Mr Hope winked at Betty. "Oh, I should think so," he said. "Just this once."

Mandy felt like cheering. This had got to be one of the best days of her life.

8

Blackie solves a problem

A day or so later the kittens were well and truly settled at Animal Ark.

As a special treat Mr and Mrs Hope let Mandy keep them up in her bedroom. They had a brand-new wooden box that Grandad had made and James's mum had sent over a special blanket. The box stood against the warm radiator.

Mrs Hope found six little dishes for their milk. Mandy insisted they each had one of their own – and Mr Hope had found a litter tray for them to use while they were there.

Mandy gave all the kittens names. She wrote the names down in her kitten diary.

She called the largest black kitten "Cheeky".

"Black with a tiny ginger tip to her tail," Mandy wrote.

She studied the others. "Sam," she said

suddenly. "That's a good name too." She wrote that down. "All black," she put, "with a tiny ginger spot over one eye."

She went on gazing at the kittens. They were rolling around on her bedside rug pretending to fight. They looked full of health. Their eyes were bright and their tummies were quite chubby now and full of milk.

"Ginger," she said. "That sounds pretty good." She wrote it down. Then "Carrots" because the colour of the kitten's fur reminded Mandy of the lovely orange carrots Grandad grew in his vegetable garden.

Mandy thought about the residents of the home. She felt sure they would like the name "Carrots" too.

There were two kittens left. Both were black *and* ginger. The smaller of the two was very lively. He had already managed to climb up Mandy's quilt and on to her bed.

"I know," Mandy said suddenly. "Clown . . . that's a brilliant name for a naughty boy like you. And . . ." Then she remembered the old man at the home who said he didn't like cats. "George," Mandy decided. She wrote it down then looked at the page filled with names. "He's bound to like you if you're named after him."

Mandy went to pick up George. She gave him a cuddle and rubbed his soft fur against her cheek.

"There you are," she said feeling satisfied. "Now you've all got names. I can't wait to introduce you to your new owners."

Mandy felt a pang of sadness. She would really miss the kittens. Having them here was like having her very own pets. Then she smiled to herself. Six kittens were rather a lot. They needed much more space than her small bedroom. Della would still need help so that meant Mandy would still see a lot of the kittens and they would always be very special to her.

A few days after that Mr Hope declared the kittens were fit to go to their new home.

"We'll take them on Saturday morning," he told Mandy.

Mandy had been very busy looking after the kittens. She fed them and cleaned out their tray every morning before she went to school. She rushed home after school to feed them again. Then she had a play with them before tea. As they no longer had their mother to groom them, Mandy did it instead. She found a little soft brush and groomed their fur.

Each day Mandy checked their ears to make sure they were clean. Then she bathed their eyes gently with cotton wool.

Last thing every night, Mandy wrote in her diary. There were lots of things for her to write about. In fact, it was almost full up.

In the diary were the names and details of all the kittens. Mandy had written down what they liked to eat and what games they liked to play. She also wrote what happened each day.

On the day before the kittens were ready to go to their new home Mandy made her last entry.

It had been six days since Mr Greene had

left the kittens at Betty's sanctuary.

Mandy put . . .

<u>Kitten Day 6</u>
The last day at Animal Ark.
Morning: I gave Cheeky, Carrots, Ginger, George, Clown and Sam their breakfast. Cheeky pinched some of Ginger's. George pinched some of Sam's. Clown pushed his bowl under the chair and ate his there. He doesn't like the other kittens watching him eat his breakfast.

Evening: I gave the kittens a special wash and brush up. They start their new jobs as pat–cats tomorrow at Westmoor House. George was naughty. He ran under my dressing–table and would not come out. Clown climbed on my bed and got lost under the quilt. James came and almost sat on top of him. The others were good. I know I'll feel sad when the kittens have gone.

★　★　★

Mandy made a special copy of the diary for Della and the old people.

She hoped her diary would be one of the most interesting ones in the class. After all, who else would have had six kittens to write about?

On Saturday morning Mrs Hope came upstairs to Mandy's bedroom. She was carrying a big basket with a wire door on the front. It was a special basket for carrying cats and kittens.

All the kittens were asleep in their box. Mandy felt very proud as she gently took them out, one by one. They were all sleek and healthy. They yawned and stretched then sat up and began washing themselves. It was as if they knew they were going somewhere special.

Mandy took their blanket from the box and put it in the basket. She knew they would like to have their own blanket in their new home.

She put the kittens inside the basket. All except Clown. He had disappeared as usual.

Mandy lay on her tummy and looked under the bed. Clown was there playing with a pencil that Mandy had dropped.

Mandy stretched out her arm and picked him up. "Trust you!" she said. She kissed his tiny nose. Then she put him carefully into the basket and closed the wire door.

Mandy picked up the basket and took it downstairs. Mrs Hope followed with the wooden box.

Mr Hope was in the kitchen getting ready to go out on a call. "All set then?" he asked.

"Yep," Mandy said. She couldn't hide the sadness in her voice. "You'd better say goodbye to our kitten crowd."

Mr Hope peered into the basket. "Well, Mandy," he said. "They look splendid. You've certainly made a good job of looking after them."

"Thanks, Dad." Mandy sighed. "I'm really going to miss them."

Mr Hope gave her a hug. "I'm sure you'll still see lots of them."

Mandy managed a smile. "Yes, I know

Shouting, Mandy ran after him. "Leave!" she commanded when she caught him halfway through the bathroom door.

Blackie wagged his tail.

Mandy frowned and tried to sound angry. "Leave!" she said again.

Blackie suddenly dropped the teddy at her feet. She rubbed his head. "Good boy!"

"Good boy!" James gasped. "When has Blackie ever been good?"

"You must give him lots of praise," Mandy said in a knowing voice.

"What, even when he steals your things?" James said.

"No, when he gives them back." Mandy laughed. "Come on, Mum will wonder what's happened."

When they got back downstairs, Mrs Hope was still in the surgery. Mandy went to put the basket into the back of the car. It was then that she saw the door of the basket had swung open.

The kittens were nowhere to be seen!

"Oh, James!" Mandy gasped in horror.

She spun round. How could six kittens disappear in such a short time? Now what were they going to do?

Blackie was sniffing at the blanket. Then, nose to the ground, he headed off into the shrubbery.

"Quick!" James ran after him. "I bet he can smell them."

Mandy followed. They could hear Blackie snuffling around under one of the bushes.

Mandy bent down. There, playing with some dead leaves, were two of the kittens. She heaved a sigh of relief. She couldn't think *what* she would have done if they were lost for ever.

"Good boy!" she said to Blackie. She reached out and picked up two of the kittens, Cheeky and Ginger. "I've got two, James," she called.

Mandy put the kittens in the basket and shut the door firmly.

James had run down the path. "Here's George," he called, scooping the mottled kitten up into his arms. He suddenly dived to one side. "And here's Sam." Sam was sitting at the bottom of the tall tree by the gate. He had been playing with a feather he had found on the path. James scooped him up too and returned them both to the basket.

Mandy was looking round. "Thank goodness," she said. "Now . . . two more, Carrots and Clown. Oh, James, where have they gone?"

Blackie had run round the side of the house. Suddenly they heard the thud of something hitting the ground. Mandy and James looked at one another then ran round after him. If anyone could find the two missing kittens, it was Blackie.

But Blackie was standing with his paws on the dustbin. He had reached up and knocked the plastic lid off with his nose. It was one of his favourite tricks.

Mandy grabbed his collar. "The kittens won't be in there, silly," she said. She pushed Blackie forward. "Find them, please, Blackie."

Just then she heard a small miaow. She

spun round, frowning. Where on earth was it coming from?

James ran to look in the shed. The door was shut tight so he came back to Mandy.

"They won't be in there . . ." he began.

Mandy held her finger to her lips. "Shh."

Mandy heard the kitten again. The sound seemed to be coming from somewhere near her feet.

Then the dustbin lid began to move. Mandy jumped back in surprise. James stared at it, wide-eyed. The lid moved again. Blackie gave a little yelp and crept away, his tail between his legs.

Then Mandy gave a shout. She knew exactly what was making the lid move. She picked it up. There, underneath, looking dazed, crouched Carrots. The lid must have fallen on top of him when Blackie knocked it off.

"Poor old Carrots," James said.

Mandy picked up the kitten and hugged him to her. She quickly felt his back and legs. "He's OK," she said. "Blackie, you're

the cleverest dog in the world." Blackie was sitting by the hedge looking sorry for himself.

"And the naughtiest." James gave his dog a hug. Blackie wriggled out of his grasp and ran to the front gate.

They quickly searched the back garden but there was no sign of the last kitten. They hurried back to the basket and put Carrots inside.

Mrs Hope came out of the surgery door with the kittens' box.

"Sorry I've been so long," she said. "I had to take a telephone call. Come on, let's get going."

Mandy quickly explained what had happened.

"Clown's still missing," she said. "We can't possibly go until we've found him."

"He can't have gone far." Mrs Hope looked round. "Maybe he went back indoors?"

Mandy shook her head. "He couldn't have. The door's been shut all the time."

James had followed Blackie back to the

bottom of the tree. Blackie looked up and suddenly began barking.

"Over here!" James shouted.

James was looking up into the branches. He pointed. "Up there," he said.

Mandy gasped. She suddenly felt wobbly at the knees. There, sitting on one of the highest branches was Clown, the naughtiest kitten of them all!

9

The best presents

"Well, well, what *have* we got here?"

Mandy turned to see Mrs McFarlane standing behind her. She was gazing up into the tree.

"A kitten," Mandy told her. "Stuck."

"Better call the fire brigade," Mrs McFarlane said. "You'll never get him down on your own."

"I think we should try first," Mrs Hope said. She went round the back to get a ladder. But when she put it up against the tree it only reached halfway.

By now, other village folk had arrived. Walter Pickard had been on his way to the shop. He stood gazing up into the tree shaking his head.

"My, my," he said. "That *is* a long way up."

Then Grandad arrived on his bike.

"What's going on, Emily?" he asked Mrs Hope.

When she told him he burst out laughing. "Mandy Hope," he said. "What-ever next!"

"It's not funny, Grandad," Mandy said, close to tears.

Grandad stood with his chin in his hand. "Maybe you could persuade him to climb down?"

Mandy shook her head. "He's too scared."

Mandy's teacher, Mrs Todd, drew up in her car. She got out to see what all the fuss was about.

"Well, Mandy," she said, when Mrs Hope explained. "This is going to be something to put in your diary."

Mandy was growing more and more anxious. Everyone was talking about Clown but no one was *doing* anything.

"I think we *had* better get the fire brigade," Mrs Hope said at last. "I'll explain to them on the phone." She disappeared indoors.

Mandy stood gazing up at Clown. He was crouched on a fragile branch looking very frightened indeed. She didn't think she could bear it if he made a sudden movement and fell off. "Please, please stay still, Clown," she whispered. "We'll get you down, I know we will."

James was crouched down, his face buried in Blackie's neck. It seemed he couldn't bear to look either.

It wasn't long before the fire engine came roaring along the village street towards them. It drew up outside Animal Ark.

Six burly fire-fighters piled out.

"Right," the chief said. "Where's this kitten?"

Mandy pointed. "Up there," she said anxiously. "He's very scared. Please can you get him down?"

The chief tipped his helmet back on his head. He gazed upwards. Then he made a salute. "Don't you worry, young lady," he said. "We'll do our best."

The fire-fighters got their long ladder from the top of the engine. With a screech and a clang they put it up against the tree.

Higher and higher it went, until it almost reached the branch where Clown was crouched. One of the fire-fighters began to climb. When he got to the top he stretched out his arms.

Mandy held her breath. The fire-fighter's fingers were centimetres away from Clown. The kitten gave a small miaow and moved backwards.

By now, quite a crowd had gathered. Everyone gave a gasp.

Then the fire-fighter shook his head and began to climb back down.

"I'm sorry,' he said when he reached the bottom. "That branch is too fragile to hold my weight. I'm not sure we're going to be able to get him."

Everyone began talking among themselves.

"We'll have to call for a longer ladder," the chief was saying. "I can't risk one of my men having an accident."

Mandy stared up at Clown. It could be ages before another ladder arrived. She had to *do* something. If the branch wouldn't hold the fire-fighter's weight, maybe it would hold hers?

Mandy looked at James and held her finger to her lips. His mouth fell open when he saw what Mandy intended to do. James began to shake his head. "Mandy, no!" he hissed.

Blackie lay down and hid his face in his paws.

But Mandy had made up her mind. She was going to rescue Clown herself.

She began to climb the ladder. Up and up until she felt she might almost touch the sky. She didn't dare look down. Right at the top she stepped carefully on to Clown's branch.

"Now don't move," she told him sternly. "Stay where you are and I can reach you."

Mandy clung on for dear life. Her heart was thudding like a drum. She crawled slowly along the branch towards the kitten. Then she stretched out her hand and scooped him up. The kitten clung to her, glad to be rescued at last.

Below, Mandy heard Mrs Hope shout. "Mandy, what on earth are you doing!" She had been talking to Grandad with her back to the ladder and had only just noticed what Mandy was up to.

But Mandy was already on her way down. When she reached the bottom everyone cheered.

Mrs Hope took hold of her arm. "Mandy, you shouldn't have done that. You might have fallen!" She looked angry.

Mandy hung her head. Now she was back down, she realised just how danger-ous her climb had been. "I'm sorry, Mum. I couldn't leave poor little Clown up there any longer."

Mrs Hope put her arm round Mandy and gave her a hug.

"Don't you ever do anything like that again," she said.

Soon Clown was tucked safely back in with the other kittens.

Mandy thanked the fire-fighters. She watched as the fire engine roared off down the main street. It wasn't every day that there was an exciting rescue in the sleepy village.

When the kitten basket was safely in the back of the car they set off for Westmoor House.

"You'd better leave Blackie in the car," Mrs Hope told James when they arrived at Westmoor House. "He'll only cause havoc. We've had enough trouble for one day!"

"OK." James wound down the window a little so that Blackie had some fresh air.

One of Della's helpers opened the door. "Come in, come in," he said. "Everyone's waiting."

Mandy felt excited as they marched along the hall towards the big sitting-room at the end. She and James carried the basket between them. With six chubby kittens inside it was quite heavy.

In the sitting-room everyone stopped talking and turned to look at them. One man went to turn off the television.

"Hurrah!" someone called. "They're here!"

Mandy smiled and nodded. Della rose from a chair by the fire and came over.

"We've all been so excited," she said. She peered into the basket then drew in her breath. "Oh, they're so sweet! Look, everyone!"

Mandy put the basket down. She opened the door a fraction and took out one of the kittens.

"This is Sam." She took him over and gave him to a lady sitting by the window.

Then she took out another one. "This is Carrots," she announced.

Everyone smiled and laughed. "What a good name," one of the men called. He held out his arms. "Can I hold him?"

James took Carrots and placed him in the old man's arms.

"I've got a cat too," James whispered.

"What's his name?" the old gentleman asked.

"Benji," said James. "He's big and fluffy. I've got a puppy as well. He's called Blackie."

"I used to have a dog," the old man told

him. "But a cat will do just as well." He smiled down at Carrots. The kitten was purring and rubbing his face against the old man's woolly cardigan.

"This is Cheeky," Mandy bent down to take the black kitten from the basket.

Cheeky wriggled and jumped out of her arms. She scampered over to Mrs Brown and began to climb up the leg of her stool. Della went to rescue her. She put her on Mrs Brown's lap. Cheeky curled up and began to purr gently. The old lady's face lit up as she stroked the kitten's soft fur.

"Thank you, Mandy," she said. "Cheeky is going to be my favourite."

"And this is Clown." Mandy lifted the kitten out. Clown seemed no worse for his ordeal in the tree. "He's *really* bad," Mandy said. She looked round. "Who wants him?"

A dozen arms were outstretched. "Give him to Tom," Della suggested.

Mandy took the kitten over to Tom. Tom was sitting with his back to everyone. Mandy tapped him gently on the shoulder.

"Would you like to hold this one?" she said softly.

Tom mumbled something that Mandy could not hear.

"Please," she said. "You'll feel much better. He'll make you laugh, honestly."

The old man turned slowly. The frown fell from his face when he saw the pretty kitten.

Mandy put Clown gently into Tom's lap. Tom turned away again and softly stroked Clown's head. Mandy could see Clown was going to be Tom's best friend. She smiled to herself and went back to the basket.

There were two kittens left.

"This is Ginger," she said taking her out. Ginger was the laziest of all the kittens. She opened one sleepy eye and yawned.

"I'll have her," said Dolly.

Mrs Hope took Ginger over. The kitten took one look at Dolly then curled round on her lap and went fast asleep. Dolly smiled. She lay back in her chair and closed her eyes too.

"Now . . ." Mandy took George out. She went over to the old man who didn't like cats. "He's named after you, George," she said, gazing at the old man.

The old man shook his head and turned away. "Smells!" he said.

"No, he doesn't," Mandy said indignantly. "He's clean and beautiful. Look at him."

The old man looked at Mandy. Then he looked at the kitten. He shrugged his shoulders. "If no one else wants him . . ."

"I do," a voice came from the corner. "I'll have the little fellow."

George snatched the kitten from Mandy's arms. "No, you won't," he said. "He's mine!"

"Oh, dear," Mrs Hope said. "I hope they're not going to quarrel over them."

Della laughed. "I'm sure they'll sort it out." She turned to Mandy and James. "They're beautiful. Thank you so much, you two."

Mandy took her diary from her pocket. She gave it to Della. "This is for you," she said shyly.

Della opened the diary. As well as writing all about them, Mandy had drawn a little picture of each of the cats.

Della drew in her breath.

"It's lovely, Mandy." She took the diary across to Mrs Brown. "Look at this!"

Soon the diary was being passed around. There were "oohs" and "ahhs" from everyone.

"Did you have a nice party?" Mandy asked Mrs Brown.

"Yes, thank you, dear. It was lovely," the old lady told her.

"Did you have lots of presents?"

"Quite a few," Mrs Brown said. "But these kittens are the best present of all."

Mrs Hope looked at her watch. "I'm afraid we've got to go. I've got some calls to make."

"We'll come up tomorrow and help feed them," Mandy said as they made their way to the front door.

"That would be lovely, Mandy," Della said. "Although I've got a feeling there are going to be plenty of willing hands to look after our new family. You've made a lot of people very happy."

"No," Mandy said. "It's the *kittens* who are going to make them happy!"

On the way home, James sat in the back seat with Blackie. "You don't think they'd like a pat-puppy as well, do you?" he joked, struggling to stop the puppy from chewing the seat belt.

Mrs Hope chuckled. "Not one like Blackie, I shouldn't think. They would never cope!"

10

The winner

At school the following Monday everyone was talking about their diaries and the things they had put in them.

"I didn't have anything exciting to write," one of the boys said. "All I did was go to school, eat my dinner and watch telly."

"I went to my auntie's," someone else said.

"My brother broke his leg playing football," a friend of Mandy's told her. "So I wrote all about that."

"I went to Walton and got a new pair of shoes," another friend said.

"I went on a train through the Channel Tunnel," someone said. "It was great."

At last the time came for the class to read out their diaries. Mandy realised she had found so much to cram into hers it might take the whole lesson to read out.

When Mandy's turn came she stood up and cleared her throat.

"Kitten Diary," she said in a loud voice. For some reason she didn't feel nervous any more. "One week in the life of six kittens."

"Kitten Day 1 . . ."

When she had finished there was silence for a minute. Then everyone clapped.

Mandy blushed and sat down quickly.

"Very good, Mandy," Mrs Todd said. She looked at a boy called Paul Jackson, "Now, Paul, your turn."

When everyone had read their diaries,

Mrs Todd said, "Excellent everyone. Now, I want you all to write down on a piece of paper whose diary you thought was the best."

Mrs Todd waited a few minutes then went round collecting the votes. She sat at her desk counting. Then she looked up. She had a broad smile on her face.

"The winner is . . . Mandy Hope. Well done, Mandy!"

Mandy went red as everyone clapped again.

Mrs Todd opened her desk and took out a bag. "Come and get your first prize, Mandy."

After school Mandy rushed out to show James her prize. It was a book about animals of the rainforests.

"Oooh!" James turned to a picture of a tiger. "I wouldn't like to have to look after one of those."

"I would," Mandy said jumping on her bike. "I'd love it!"

A warm breeze was blowing as Mandy and James raced across the green. The houses and shops glowed in the afternoon sunshine.

Mandy said goodbye to James at his gate and headed off towards Animal Ark.

She felt sad as she wheeled her bike up the brick path. There wouldn't be any kittens waiting for her today. Mandy knew she would miss them terribly. Then her heart lifted. She would be able to go to Westmoor House to see the kittens whenever she wanted. She knew they would be well looked after and, after all, she did know lots of pets that were *almost* her own.

Mandy pushed open the door of Animal Ark and went inside.

An envelope lay on the kitchen table. It was addressed to Mandy. When she opened it she saw it was a card from everyone at Westmoor House.

"Thank you for our pat-cats, Mandy," it said. "They are all lovely. Come and see us again soon."

Mandy sat back in the chair. She smiled to herself. There was no doubt about it. Finding such a loving home for a whole crowd of kittens had been one of the best things she had ever done.